Young Wizards

by

Michael Lawrence

5

Illustrated by Chris Mould

You do not need to read this page – just get on with the book!

First published in 2008 in Great Britain by
Barrington Stoke Ltd
18 Walker St, Edinburgh, EH3 7LP

www.barringtonstoke.co.uk

ISBN: 978-1-84299-539-6

Printed in Great Britain by Bell & Bain Ltd

AUTHOR ID

Name: Michael Lawrence

Likes: The idea of doing nothing at all. If only I had the time.

Dislikes: There isn't enough room on the page for me to write them all down!

3 words that best describe me:
Dashing, daring, strong (sadly, three lies).

A secret that not many people know:
I am a Young Wizard in disguise.

ILLUSTRATOR ID

Name: Chris Mould

Likes: Running for miles with my iPod, boxing, eating! Reading, frosty mornings, taking photos, writing and drawing, days out with my family, pastry and olives!

Dislikes: Bad manners, traffic, bills, slippers, litter, buying petrol, empty bank accounts and marzipan.

3 words that best describe me:
Mad. Unusual. Different (well, that's what my mum says).

A secret that not many people know:
I love cooking and I cook every day.

For Erin

Contents

Chapter 1
Strange Things

Let me start by telling you that there was no magic on the Wizard Lea Estate. Wizard Lea was as un-magical as any housing estate can be. Oh, it was nice enough. The houses were modern, the gardens were neat, and most of the cars that stood in the drive-ways or at the kerbs weren't very old. But of real magic there wasn't a drop.

And this was the very thing that had drawn Mr and Mrs Pertinax to it. Well, that and its name, of course.

"The Wizard Lea Estate," they said when they heard of it. "Oh, we *must* move there."

So, almost a year ago, that's what they did.

Mr and Mrs Pertinax had three children: a girl and two boys. Ellie, the girl, was the eldest. The boys were twins, called Brin and Arlo. This story begins the Friday morning that Brin and Arlo became eleven years and six months of age.

Now, becoming eleven years and six months is nothing special. For one thing, as it's slap-bang between birthdays eleven and twelve you don't get presents and cards. The twins might not have minded this if it hadn't been the day before Ellie's thirteenth birthday. The day she would be getting all the things that they would not.

"Why the long faces?" their mother asked when they went down to breakfast that morning.

"Want a birthday tomorrow," Brin said glumly.

"Well, you can't have a birthday tomorrow," she replied. "Anyway, I think eleven and a half is quite old enough for two growing boys to be getting on with."

As she said this, she looked at her husband, who was eating his toast and reading the morning paper. He looked worried.

Mr Pertinax said, "Apart from being jealous of your sister's birthday tomorrow, do you two feel ... all right?"

"No," said Arlo. "We're fed up."

"Not yet, you're not," said Mum. "Sit down and eat your breakfast."

They sat down, and while they ate, Ellie smirked at them across the table. *Tomorrow,* the smirk seemed to say, *I'll have a birthday and you won't.* It was because of that smirk that, after breakfast, Brin and Arlo made up their minds to give their sister a very un-special present tomorrow.

They found it in the cupboard under the stairs, at the back of a shelf covered in cobwebs. It was the most un-special present they could think of. Their late grandmother's dustpan and brush. It was so old and worn that it hadn't been used for years. "Tee-hee," they said, as they sneaked the dustpan and brush upstairs. In their room, they wrapped it in some left-over Christmas paper and put it under one of their beds.

Finding and wrapping the un-special present cheered the twins up so much that when their friends called for them, they were quite happy to go to school, for a change.

Mr and Mrs Pertinax, still very worried, watched them go.

****

It was at school that morning that strange things started to happen.

The first strange thing happened in Maths. Mr Choi had set the class a test, and had filled the board with sums that he wanted everyone to try and work out before the end of the lesson.

"Is there a reward for anyone who gets them all right, sir?" Harry Pooter asked.

"Yes," said Mr Choi. "A shocked grin from me. Go on, now, impress me!"

The class had been working on the sums for about five minutes when the deputy head looked in. There was a phone call for Mr Choi in the office. Mr Choi told the class to keep working while he was away, and left them to it.

For a minute or two after he'd gone, they carried on working, but then someone threw a paper-clip. Then someone else threw an exercise book. And in another minute, almost everyone was throwing things, standing on chairs, or fighting under the desks.

Arlo grinned. "This is better than doing rotten sums," he said.

"Anything's better than sums," agreed Brin. He waved his hands at the board like a stage magician, and hissed, "Vanish, sums!"

And that was when the first strange thing happened. The sums dribbled down the board,

ran off the bottom, and fell into a heap on the floor, where they faded to minus nothing.

Brin and Arlo just stared – first at the blank board, then at one another.

"Uh?" they said.

Then someone else saw it. "What happened to the sums?"

And someone else. "Where did they go?"

Then everyone looked, and wondered the same thing. They were still wondering when Mr Choi returned and asked crossly who had rubbed his sums off. When no one admitted to having done it, he gave the whole class extra Maths homework.

Chapter 2
Stranger Still

The next strange thing happened in Art. Mrs Mellor had set up a still-life for everyone to draw. It was of a bowl of fruit, a water jug, some dried flowers, and a folded scarf. Some of the girls thought it quite an interesting still-life, but few of the boys did. Arlo waggled an annoyed hand and said that he wished Mrs Mellor would let them draw monsters instead.

"Today, class," Mrs Mellor said a moment later, "I want you all to draw monsters."

"Monsters?" someone said in amazement.

"And I want to see some really *horrible* ones please," Mrs Mellor added. "Is that understood?"

Puzzled as they were, everyone was soon hard at work drawing the most horrible monsters they could imagine.

They drew blood-sucking vampires. They drew snarling were-wolves. They drew demons with horns and claws. They drew staring zombies. They drew aliens with tentacles. They drew screaming skulls. They drew giant gorillas beating their chests. They drew ... well, you name it, as long as it was really horrible, the class drew it. It was the best time they'd ever had in Art.

After twenty minutes, Mrs Mellor began walking round looking at the drawings – and she was *horrified*.

"What are you all doing?" she cried.

"We're drawing monsters, Miss."

"Why are you drawing monsters? I told you to draw my still-life."

"No, you didn't. You said we had to draw monsters."

"Oh, really! Why would I say something like that?"

"Dunno, Miss, but you did."

At the end of the lesson, Brin and Arlo left the Art room in a daze.

"What happened back there?" said Brin.

"I don't even want to *think* about it," said Arlo.

It was during lunch break that the third strange thing happened. Most of the school ate lunch in the canteen. School meals were quite healthy these days, and most of the students liked them. But Brin and Arlo were among those who liked kinds of food other than curry, nut cutlets, salad, and vegetarian lasagne. Brin waved his hand in despair at the serving counters.

"Why can't it be beans, chips and burgers, and treacle pudding and chocolate sauce, like we *used* to have?" he said.

He'd hardly finished speaking when a gasp went up from the children in front of them. They craned their necks to see what had made everyone gasp, and saw the food that had been put on some of the plates.

"Beans, chips, burgers, treacle pudding and chocolate sauce!" cried Brin.

"And all on the same plate!" said Arlo.

As well as being pretty confused about this, some of the students didn't fancy such a mixture, but Brin and Arlo took the plates that two of them didn't want and carried them to a table well away from everyone else. While teachers and canteen staff scratched their heads about the shocking change that had come over the food, the twins ate up gladly. Chips went quite well with treacle pudding, they found. And as for baked beans in chocolate sauce ...

"These things that are happening," said Arlo as they tucked in. "You don't think they're anything to do with us, do you?"

"Us?" said Brin.

15

"Well, think about it. What was the first weird thing that happened?"

"The sums vanished from Mr Choi's board."

"Yes. After you wished they would."

"Just a fluke."

"And what about Art? Mrs Mellor set up a still-life, then told us to draw monsters instead – right after I wished we could. And she didn't even remember *telling* us to draw them!"

"I don't get it," said Brin.

"Me neither," said Arlo. "But this food's great!"

****

The main lesson after lunch was Games. For this, the girls went off with Mrs Cork and the boys went with Mr Antony. The school sports day was coming up, so they had to practice the events they would be taking part in, such as the long-jump, the high-jump, and the relay race. The twins, being as good or as bad as one another at everything, were getting ready for the 100m sprint with a number of other boys.

"I hate running," Brin grumbled as everyone got into position at the starting blocks. "Wish we could speed it up and get it over with."

"Maybe we can," said Arlo.

"How?"

"Well, if we really can make weird things happen ..."

Because the twins thought so much alike, Brin knew exactly what he meant. He smiled, and the two of them said in a whisper, "When Mr Antony blows the whistle we're going to run like *race-horses!*" And as they said it they waggled their fingers as though making magic.

"Ready, lads?" Mr Antony said.

Then he blew his whistle, and all the boys at the starting blocks bent over, put their hands on the ground, and galloped off like *race-horses!*

"Maybe we should have just said run fast, not like horses," panted Brin as they sped over the finishing line.

"Still," said Arlo as they stood upright again, "that proves it. It's us that's making the weird stuff happen!"

"Yeah." Brin grinned from ear to ear. "Fantastic!"

Chapter 3
Truths About Magic

After school, at home, the twins told Ellie all that had happened during the day. She didn't believe a word at first. But then a friend phoned to say that her sister (who was in Brin and Arlo's class) had told her about the vanishing sums, the Art teacher telling her students to draw monsters, the change that came over the food in the canteen, and the boys galloping like horses round the playing field.

"All right, so some crazy stuff went down today," Ellie said after she'd hung up. "But that doesn't mean you two made it happen."

"I'm afraid it does," said a voice behind them. Their dad had just come in with the shopping.

"Do you know what this is all about?" Arlo asked him.

"Oh, I know all right," said Mr Pertinax.

"Tell us then," said Brin.

"I will. When your mother gets in."

When Mrs Pertinax came home from work, he took her to one side and told her what he'd heard the children talking about.

"It's happened," Mrs Pertinax said, going pale. "Just as we feared it might."

Mr Pertinax nodded glumly.

When the evening meal was dished up and the family was sitting at the table, Mr Pertinax began his tale.

"As you know," he said, "we moved to the village of Witch Haven just after Ellie was born. We moved there in the hope of living a normal life, which hadn't always been easy. You see, I come from a long line of wizards."

"Wizards?" all three children said together.

"Wizards. In the olden days, Pertinax wizards were in great demand. We were hired by kings and great lords to protect them and bring about the defeat of their enemies. But that was then. There's not much demand for wizards in the 21st century, apart from in stories and the cinema. It's a bit tricky sometimes."

"Tricky?" said Brin.

"Not to do magic. I try to keep it to myself, but when you're a born wizard, the magic has a way of coming out every now and then whether you mean it to or not."

"Pull the other one, Dad," said Ellie. "You, a wizard? Ha!"

Her mother frowned. "Ellie," she said. "Every word of what your father says is true."

"So how come we've never seen him do magic then?"

"Because he's gone out of his way to keep it from you, that's why."

"Keep it from us?" said Arlo. "Why? Magic is so cool!" Unlike Ellie, he had no problem believing their parents.

Nor did Brin. "Show us some magic, Dad," he said.

"I suppose I must, to prove it to you," said Mr Pertinax. His eyes settled on a vase of flowers on a small table under the window. He frowned, winked, and waved a hand. The flowers, the vase and the table turned into a coat-stand.

"Woh!" said Brin and Arlo, and even Ellie's mouth fell open.

"Simple party trick," their father said. "But when you can do such things with ease, you have to be on your toes all the time in case you make something happen while you're thinking of something else."

"Which is what caused our problems at Witch Haven," his wife said. "A few bits of magic done by mistake – a brilliant rainbow springing up on a cloudy day, someone's nose

growing when they tell lies – and people begin to wonder who's to blame."

"Is that why we had to move?" Brin asked.

"It is. Gossip started to go around about us and we were getting odd looks in the street. Then, finally ... you remember the night the brick came through the window?"

At the time, Mr and Mrs Pertinax had told the children that yobs had been throwing bricks at a number of houses in the village.

"You don't mean it was only our window that got broken?" Ellie said.

"I do," her mother said. "What you didn't notice – we hid it so you wouldn't worry – was that there was a note round the brick."

"A note? What did it say?"

"It said, 'Go home, aliens'."

Brin frowned. "Aliens? We're not aliens."

"We were different, which is the same thing to some people. After that, we knew we had to start again somewhere else. So we moved here. But after today ..."

"After today what?" Ellie asked.

"Well, it seems that I've passed on the wizard gene to the boys," Mr Pertinax said. "We hoped I hadn't. It misses the odd Pertinax male, you see, but events at school today show that it was a forlorn hope."

"You mean we *did* do magic?" Arlo said.

"I'm afraid you did."

The twins stared at one another.

"I don't get it," said Ellie. "If this is true, why did it start today? I mean, why *today*?"

Mrs Pertinax explained. "If the wizard gene is going to come out, it starts the day a male of the line reaches eleven years and six months exactly. That's why we were nervous this morning. It turns out that we were right to be."

"I wonder if they can be taught to control it?" Mr Pertinax said, looking at the twins. "Learn not to make magic when there's anyone about, I mean."

"But making magic would be fun!" cried Brin.

"It could also get us noticed," said Mrs Pertinax. "There would be photos in the papers, and we'd be on TV. People wouldn't leave us alone. They would try and drive us out, like last time."

"We have to give it a try," Mr Pertinax said. "When we've finished eating, you boys will go with me to the park, where I'll try to show you how to keep your magic to yourselves."

"It's not fair!" Ellie said suddenly. "Why should these two be able to do magic and not me? I'm the eldest."

"Ellie, listen to me," her mother said. "Magic is not a blessing. In today's world it's more trouble than it's worth. Even in the past, people who used it weren't always treated with respect. Take witches, for example."

"Witches?"

"Many of them were drowned or burnt at the stake."

Ellie stuck her lower lip out. "Wish I was a witch," she said.

"Don't say that!" Mrs Pertinax said sharply. "Hope to become a normal teenager and nothing more."

"Normal's boring," Ellie grumbled.

"At least people don't throw bricks at normal teenagers," her dad said.

"Most of the time," said Mrs Pertinax.

Chapter 4
Daisies and Dragons

Much of the park was open grass-land. There were trees, of course, and bushes, and flowerbeds, and there was also a small lake, but that was about it. This made it the perfect place to practise magic. As luck would have it, there was no one else there that evening.

"I think the best thing," Mr Pertinax said to the twins, "is for me to show you the right way to make magic. Then you'll have some idea of what not to do when there are people about. Now where shall we start ...?"

He looked about him and saw that the grass around a nearby oak tree was thick with little white daisies.

"You see those daisies?" he said. "What I'd like you to do is make them grow. I mean *really* grow."

"What for?" Brin asked.

"To see if you can."

"Can't we do something else? Something interesting, like, say, make thunder. Or lightning."

"All in good time," said Mr Pertinax. "For now, let's see if you can make daisies grow."

"How do we do it?" asked Arlo.

"Well, to start with, you point at them."
Mr Pertinax held up the index finger of his
right hand. "This is a wizard's pointing
finger," he said. "The rest of the fingers are
used to make other kinds of magic, but for
the moment let's see what you can do with
this one."

Brin and Arlo pointed at the daisies round
the oak tree.

"Now close your eyes and focus on
making them grow really tall," Mr Pertinax
said.

"We didn't focus when we made that stuff
happen at school," said Brin.

"Maybe not, but you weren't in control
then either. Control is very important. If
your hands and minds aren't focused on the
same thing, there can be odd side-effects."

The boys closed their eyes, tried to focus, and in half a minute some of the daisies started to grow.

"Oh, well done, Arlo!" Mr Pertinax said.

Both boys opened their eyes.

"How do you know it was him and not me who did that?" Brin asked.

"I know because you weren't holding your finger still and you kept peeking."

"I'll try again then."

Brin closed his eyes once more, but he was so excited by what he might do with these new powers that he couldn't keep the fingers of his other hand still. And ...

"Oh, no!" cried Mr Pertinax.

Brin's eyelids jumped back. "What's up?"

"Look at the sky!"

It had become dark and grim, and as they looked a bolt of white lightning zigged out of it and struck the oak tree. There was a mighty crack, and a branch snapped and crashed to the ground.

"Well, you made your lightning after all," Mr Pertinax said. He didn't sound very pleased.

"You mean I did that?" said Brin in amazement.

"Yes. You did. And why? Because you didn't keep your fingers under control while you focused. That was very foolish of you, Brin. If there'd been anyone about, they could have been badly hurt."

Brin looked down at his feet. "Sorry, Dad."

Mr Pertinax would have said more, but he was cut short by a sharp yapping sound and a small dog – a spaniel – that ran between them and cocked its leg against the daisies, which were now a metre high.

Arlo waved the dog away. "Buzz off, you stupid mutt!"

The words were hardly out of his mouth when the dog lifted off the ground (spraying the giant daises as it did so) and its yap became a loud buzz. Then, flying through the air, it made a 'bee-line' for the lake.

"What's that dog of mine up to?" said the dog's owner, running up as it tumbled nose-first into the water.

"Looks like he wanted a paddle," Mr Pertinax said.

"From where I was standing it looked like he *flew* there!"

"Most likely it's just high spirits."

"Weird! Like those giant snap-dragons. And what about that lightning? Global warming has a lot to answer for, if you ask me!"

"What was that about snap-dragons?" Brin said as they watched the man go after his dog.

This was answered by an angry snap-snap-snap sound behind them, followed by growls and hisses. Before the boys could turn to see what was there, the grass around their feet burst into flames.

"Run, boys, run!" cried their dad, grabbing each of them by an arm.

The twins looked over their shoulders as he rushed them away. The giant daisies were giant daisies no longer. They were dragon heads on stalks – breathing fire!

"What happened to the daisies?" Arlo said.

"The dog weed on them," his father replied.

"So?"

"It was a spaniel."

"So?"

"Spaniel-widdle added to giant magic daisies changes the daisies into snap-dragons. If the dog had been a different breed, the result would have been different."

"Different how?" asked Brin.

"Well, if a wolf-hound had piddled on the daises they would have turned into enormous Venus Fly-traps, which could take your arm off. And if it had been a corgi we would now be looking at Scorpion Orchids – even more dangerous!"

"The flames are going out," Brin said, looking back.

And so they were. And the fire-breathing snap-dragons were turning back into daisies. And the daisies were shrinking back to normal size.

"I think we need to practice somewhere else," Mr Pertinax said to his sons. "Somewhere more private."

"Like where?" said Arlo.

"Like home."

****

"How did they get on?" Mrs Pertinax asked when they walked in.

"Well, we've made a start," her husband said. "But for safety's sake, the next lesson is going to be given in our own back garden."

When he and the twins had gone out to the garden, Mrs Pertinax saw her daughter's down-turned mouth.

"Now what?" she asked.

"Same thing as before," Ellie said. "They've got magic and I haven't. I want to be a wizard too."

"Girls can't be wizards," her mother said.

"Well, I never asked to be a girl."

"No, you didn't, but for your sake I hope that's all you ever are."

"What do you mean?" asked Ellie.

"I mean, don't you have homework that has to be in by Monday?"

"I'll do it on Sunday," Ellie said. "If I were a *wizard* I'd make it do itself."

"You would not," Mrs Pertinax said. "House rule: no homework to be done by magic."

She repeated this for the boys when they came in a little later.

"Oh, Mum," said Brin. "What's the point of being able to do magic if you can't use it on your homework?"

"Don't argue," she said. "You'll do your homework the same way as everyone else. I will *not* have you using magic to cheat. Are they getting the hang of it?" she asked her husband.

"Well, they're not doing badly for beginners," he replied. "Even if Arlo did turn next door's greenhouse into an enormous pink rabbit. Good thing I was there to turn it back before someone saw it."

Ellie stuck her lower lip out. "Still not fair," she muttered.

"Be positive," her mum said to her. "Think about tomorrow. The big day."

Ellie thought about tomorrow. It helped her get over her envy of her brothers. They might be young wizards, but it was she who would be getting presents in the morning!

Chapter 5
More Truths About Magic

Ellie came down next morning in as cheerful a mood as any other birthday girl. The first thing her mother did when she saw her was ask if she felt any different.

"Well, I *feel* the same as yesterday," Ellie said. "But Mum! I'm a teenager!"

"So you are, dear," her mother said, patting her hand.

As it wasn't a school morning there was no rush, so Ellie took her time opening her cards and gifts. The presents included a 1000-piece jigsaw (Ellie loved jigsaws), a watch, a chunky necklace, and an MP3 player.

"Nothing from you two, as ever," Ellie said to the twins.

"The ones from your mum and me are also from Brin and Arlo," Mr Pertinax reminded her.

"Yes, but that's only because they haven't bothered to get me anything."

The boys looked at one another. Did they have the heart to give her the 'present' they'd wrapped up yesterday morning? One of them grinned. The other one grinned back. Of course they did!

"Don't go away," they said, and scampered upstairs.

When they returned with their 'gift', Ellie began to unwrap it. Brin and Arlo could hardly contain themselves as she did so.

"Pathetic!" she said, when she saw what they'd given her.

"Oh, not that," Mrs Pertinax said. "Today of *all* days you shouldn't have given her *that*."

And suddenly, because no one saw the funny side, it didn't seem such a great joke to Brin and Arlo either. In fact, they felt rather stupid. They might have actually apologised if something hadn't happened that made their jaws drop. And not just *their* jaws. Ellie, too, stared as the brush that belonged to the battered old dustpan changed shape and size and became an old-fashioned broom with a long wooden handle and a bundle of twigs at one end.

Ellie turned on the boys, waving the broom angrily at them.

"You two think you're so clever, don't you? Well, let me tell you, this is the first and last time you're using any of that wizardy stuff on *me!*"

She turned to the main window, intending to throw the broom into the garden. But she didn't throw it. The broom threw itself, and because Ellie hadn't let go, took her with it. And once outside it flew up and up and up (taking her along for the ride), above the gardens and greenhouses and sheds and the roofs of all the houses.

Brin and Arlo rushed to the window. "How did we do that?" they gasped.

"You didn't," their father said, joining them. "She did it herself."

"How could she do it herself? She's not a young wizard."

"Not a young wizard, no. She's a young witch."

The twins gaped. "A young *witch*?"

"Just as we hoped the wizard gene would have missed you two, we hoped your gran's witch gene would miss Ellie."

"Witch gene?" said Arlo. "You mean Gran was a witch?"

"Yes."

"She didn't look like one."

"Not all witches have hooked noses and warts and cackle a lot," Mr Pertinax said. "She had her days, though, being my mother-in-law."

"But if Gran was a witch and Ellie's a witch, doesn't that mean that you're one too?" Brin said to his mother.

Mrs Pertinax shook her head. "A daughter of a witch can never become one. But a grand-daughter can. It doesn't always happen, but it *can*."

"And it clearly has in Ellie's case," said Mr Pertinax sadly.

"But she wasn't a witch yesterday," said Arlo.

"She wasn't thirteen yesterday. When a witch's grand-daughter turns thirteen, she either becomes a normal teenager or a witch like her. We would have settled for the normal teenager."

"That broom ..." Brin said, watching his sister flying around the roof-tops holding on to the handle for dear life.

"It was my mum's," said Mrs Pertinax. "When she died it changed itself into a household brush because there was no one to use it. Ellie's thirteenth birthday witch-touch must have woken it up. Made it want to stretch its twigs."

"I hope she can keep hold of it," said Mr Pertinax, staring up into the sky.

"It won't let her fall," his wife said. "It's hers now. It'll look after her."

"She's coming back!" Brin and Arlo cried.

And indeed she was. The broomstick (which Ellie was now riding rather than simply hanging on to) had swung around in the sky and was heading for the house.

They all stepped away from the window just in time. Ellie landed on the carpet with a bump. Her hair was all over the place and she was goggle-eyed, but thrilled.

"What a ride!" she said, getting off the broomstick. She turned to the twins. "Maybe I will let you do that again every now and then."

"It wasn't the boys," her mother said.

"What do you mean, it wasn't the boys? Who else could have made it happen? Unless ..." She looked at her father.

He held his hands up. "Wasn't me either."

"Ellie," Mrs Pertinax said. "We have something to tell you."

And Ellie heard how, over-night, she had become a witch. At first she was horrified.

"Me? A witch? What will my friends say?"

"Your friends mustn't know," her mother said. "It must remain a family secret. I'm sorry about this, dear. I wish the witch gene had missed you, but it hasn't, so the best thing you can do is to stay away from that broomstick and not even *think* about casting spells."

Ellie's eyes widened. "I can cast *spells?*"

"Yes, of course, but as I say, you must do nothing of the kind – not if you want to be a normal teenager."

But Ellie had stopped listening. She was muttering a spell she'd recently heard in a film about witches. At the same time she waved her hands in the direction of a framed photo of her gran.

"Hi, Ellie!" said Gran.

The picture had come to life. Gran leant out of the frame, smiling – but just for a few seconds, before she sank back and became a photo again.

Ellie grinned. "I cast a spell! And it worked!"

"We can do better than that," said Arlo.

He pointed at the TV and closed his eyes. Almost at once the TV became a full-grown tiger, eager for fresh meat. It roared and started towards them. It was a good thing that Mr Pertinax had his wits about him. He raised a hand, waggled an eyebrow, and the hungry beast became a tiger on the screen, running after a herd of deer.

"Oh, that's nothing," Ellie said. "Watch this!"

She uttered another spell, a made-up one this time, and the thousand pieces of her new jigsaw leapt out of the box and, hanging in mid-air, slotted themselves together.

"No magic in the house!" Mrs Pertinax shouted.

"Come on," said Brin. "Outside!"

As the jigsaw fell into a thousand pieces on the carpet, the young wizards and the young witch ran into the garden to see what spells they could cast, what magic they could make.

Their parents sank onto the sofa.

"Oh dear," said Mr Pertinax.

"Oh dear indeed," said Mrs Pertinax. "So much for being like everyone else. We'd better put the house up for sale. Time to move on – again!"

Barrington Stoke would like to thank all its readers for commenting on the manuscript before publication and in particular:

Caitlyn Burns
Lisa Cahill
Andrew Campbell
Craig Chapman
Courtney Cunningham
Bobbie Fifer
Matthew Gilliland
Harris Hamilton
Mhari Henderson
Christopher Johnstone
Shannon Kilpatrick
Ryan Kyle
Andrew Lynn

Jacqueline Mackie
Amy MacLean
Chloe McArthur
Steven McKinnon
Jean McKissock
Danielle McNelis
Colin Meiklem
Katie Milton
Jordanna Northorp
Hannah Parker
Margaret Wetherspoon
Caitlyn Yemm

Become a Consultant!

Would you like to give us feedback on our titles before they are published? Contact us at the email address below – we'd love to hear from you!

info@barringtonstoke.co.uk
www.barringtonstoke.co.uk

Great reads – no problem!

Barrington Stoke books are:

Great stories – from thrillers to comedy to horror, and all by the best writers around!

No hassle – fast reads with no boring bits, and a story that doesn't let go of you till the last page.

Short – the perfect size for a fast, fun read.

We use our own font and paper to make it easier to read our books. And we ask teenagers like you, who want a no-hassle read, to check every book before it's published.

That way, we know for sure that every Barrington Stoke book is a great read for everyone.

Check out **www.barringtonstoke.co.uk** for more info about Barrington Stoke and our books!

Also by Michael Lawrence...

Young Dracula
& Young Monsters

The inspiration for the
hit CBBC TV series,
"Young Dracula"

2 fab stories in 1!

Young Dracula

Count Dracula is the greatest, scariest, nastiest vampire of them all. So how come his son is the most rubbish vampire ever? Can Young Dracula show his father what he's made of?

Young Monsters

It's Lon's first day at his new school – the Dr Ffelix Ffurter School for Young Monsters! Is Lon bad enough? He'll have to be on his worst behaviour ...

You can order *Young Dracula & Young Monsters* directly from our website at
www.barringtonstoke.co.uk

If you liked this book,
why don't you try ...

Amazing

by Hilary McKay

Peter is the Quiet One. When his friends tell amazing stories, he just listens. He doesn't have adventures, or a hairy gran, or a smelly cat, or anything interesting to talk about.

Peter thinks he must be the most boring person ever.

Peter is *wrong* ...

You can order *Amazing* directly from our website at
www.barringtonstoke.co.uk

If you liked this book,
why don't you try ...

Zack Black and the Magic Dads

by Annie Dalton

Zack doesn't think he needs a dad, but his mum thinks he does. The Magic Dad website seems like the perfect way to make her happy ...

But it's not that easy. With each new Magic Dad, things go from bad to worse to crazy!

Can Zack find a new dad – or is he looking in all the wrong places?

You can order *Zack Black and the Magic Dads* directly from our website at **www.barringtonstoke.co.uk**